Dear Parents:

Congratulations! Your child is taking the first steps on an exciting journey. The destination? Independent reading!

STEP INTO READING® will help your child get there. The program offers five steps to reading success. Each step includes fun stories and colorful art or photographs. In addition to original fiction and books with favorite characters, there are Step into Reading Non-Fiction Readers, Phonics Readers and Boxed Sets, Sticker Readers, and Comic Readers—a complete literacy program with something to interest every child.

Learning to Read, Step by Step!

Ready to Read   Preschool–Kindergarten
• big type and easy words • rhyme and rhythm • picture clues
For children who know the alphabet and are eager to begin reading.

Reading with Help   Preschool–Grade 1
• basic vocabulary • short sentences • simple stories
For children who recognize familiar words and sound out new words with help.

Reading on Your Own   Grades 1–3
• engaging characters • easy-to-follow plots • popular topics
For children who are ready to read on their own.

Reading Paragraphs   Grades 2–3
• challenging vocabulary • short paragraphs • exciting stories
For newly independent readers who read simple sentences with confidence.

Ready for Chapters   Grades 2–4
• chapters • longer paragraphs • full-color art
For children who want to take the plunge into chapter books but still like colorful pictures.

STEP INTO READING® is designed to give every child a successful reading experience. The grade levels are only guides; children will progress through the steps at their own speed, developing confidence in their reading.

Remember, a lifetime love of reading starts with a single step!

Published in the United States by Random House Children's Books, a division of Penguin Random House LLC, 1745 Broadway, New York, NY 10019, and in Canada by Penguin Random House Canada Limited, Toronto.

Step into Reading, Random House, and the Random House colophon are registered trademarks of Penguin Random House LLC.

Visit us on the Web!
StepIntoReading.com
rhcbooks.com

Educators and librarians, for a variety of teaching tools, visit us at RHTeachersLibrarians.com

ISBN 978-0-593-38225-7 (trade) — ISBN 978-0-593-38226-4 (lib. bdg.)

Printed in the United States of America

10 9 8 7 6 5 4 3 2 1

BEWARE OF DOGBOT!

by Elle Stephens

based on the teleplay by Allan Neuwirth

illustrated by Erik Doescher

Random House 🏠 New York

Chuckie loves to play
with his friends: Tommy,
Susie, Phil, and Lil.
Today they are playing catch
with Tommy's doggy, Spike.

"Come on, Spike! Fetch!"
says Chuckie.
He wishes he had
a bestest doggy
friend, too.

Dogs make Chuckie's daddy sneeze,
so Chuckie can't have one
of his own.
Tommy's daddy has an idea.
He makes a robot dog
for Chuckie!

His name is Rusty.

"You two are going

to love playing together,"

says Tommy's daddy.

Later that day,

Chuckie takes Rusty

out to play.

Rusty follows

Chuckie everywhere.

"Stop following me!"

says Chuckie.

"Pet me,"

says the robot dog.

Chuckie plays hide-and-seek
with Rusty.

He hides behind a tree.

Rusty uses his robot trackers.

He finds Chuckie right away.

Chuckie plays fetch
with Rusty.
He throws a stick.
Rusty fetches it.

Rusty fetches other
things, too!

Chuckie and Rusty run
and play all day.

When Chuckie asks Rusty

to roll over,

Rusty rolls

and rolls

and rolls!

Chuckie takes Rusty
to meet his friends.
"I got a doggy, too!"
he tells them.

When Rusty has to go potty,
something bright
and colorful comes out.
Jelly beans!
Everyone loves Rusty.

After a long day,

Chuckie and Rusty go to bed.

But a loud noise outside

sets off Rusty's alarm.

It wakes everyone up!

Tommy's daddy comes over
to turn it off.
He fixes Rusty so that
he will be more helpful.

The next day,

Rusty is different.

"He's been acting all weird

and scary,"

says Chuckie.

But his friends don't think so.

They want to play bouncy ball.

Every time the ball bounces,

Rusty pushes it to Chuckie.

He is being *too* helpful.

"That's no fair!"

says Phil.

Chuckie tries to throw the ball

over Rusty.

But the robot dog kicks it

into outer space!

Tommy gets his toy Reptar.

Rusty takes that, too!

He tries to give it to Chuckie.

The babies tug it away from him,

but Reptar is ruined.

23

Just then,

Rusty grabs Chuckie.

"Time to go home,"

says the robot.

"Noooo!" says Chuckie

as they leave.

At home,

Chuckie is sad.

Rusty won't let him have fun

with his friends anymore.

His daddy says

they will give Rusty back.

25

Rusty hears.

He thinks Chuckie's daddy

is a dogcatcher.

He goes into dogcatcher mode!

Rusty's alarm turns on.

He chases Chuckie's daddy

around the house!

He chases him

into the yard

and up a tree.

"Help!" yells Chuckie.

His friends come running.

"My trusty stu-driver
to the rescue,"
says Tommy.
He opens Rusty's control panel.
Chuckie fixes the wires,
and then—

Rusty blasts off
into space!
Everyone is happy
to see him go.

Spike gives Chuckie a big lick.
"Guess I don't need my own
bestest doggy friend after all,"
says Chuckie.

"That's right,"
says Tommy.
"You've got all your
bestest friends right here!"